THE SMERALDO FLOWER

J. F. ROGERS

NOBLEBRIGHT
PUBLISHING

The Smeraldo Flower

This book is a work of fiction. Any resemblance to existing people
or places is purely coincidental.

Cover design by 100 Covers
Editing by Brilliant Cut Editing

ISBN: 978-1-955169-09-7

Published by Noblebright Publishing
Sanford, Maine
www.Noblebrightpublishing.com

To my daughter, Emily -

*Thank you for giving me an appreciation for music
with lyrics in different languages.*

A painter should begin every canvas with a wash of black, because all things in nature are dark except where exposed by the light.

— LEONARDO DA VINCI

A NEW VENTURE

Your gifts lie in the place where your values, passions and strengths meet. Discovering that place is the first step toward sculpting your masterpiece, your Life.

— MICHELANGELO

Northern Italy
THE 16TH CENTURY

The carriage bounced along the rough mountain road, steering me toward the most unusual opportunity. I braced myself as the coach tossed me about like the never-ending questions resounding in my mind.

Where would I stay? Who was Messer Viviani? What manner of man was he? What would my temporary home be like? And why were my parents so closed-lipped with the details? With each question came excitement and trepidation in equal measure.

There were too many unknowns.

Valentina, my handmaid, gasped. She sat back, holding the curtain open. "Carola, have a look."

The carriage swayed, and I fell into her lap. I righted myself and peered out her window. The massive fir trees had thinned, opening an incredible view of the valley below and the mountains beyond. I sucked in a breath as if to inhale the view to exhale onto parchment later.

This looked nothing like the Italy I knew. And the air —a refreshing earthy scent with hints of citrus. Hills dappled with fir trees rolled before me like a turbulent Verona-green sea frozen midstorm. Jagged snowcapped mountains dwarfed the tallest fir to a mere speck in comparison. Bulky clouds swept through the sky. Shadows swooped along the plains like wraiths.

"It's stunning. Perhaps the lord of the manor would allow us to return to this place so I might capture it on canvas." I'd have sketched it then, but this road didn't care for artists.

"Focus on your task so we might return to the city." Valentina's skin looked pasty.

"Are you unwell? Should I ask the driver to stop?"

She forced a smile. "And delay this lovely trip? No. The sooner we arrive, the sooner my stomach will settle."

I peeled back the curtain on my side. Nothing but trees. "What do you suppose it will be like?"

"Carola." She closed her eyes and swallowed as if holding back vomit. "As I've said countless times before... I only know our host's name, Messer Soren Viviani."

"But who is he? And why give Father such a large sum to paint a flower?"

She snapped her head my way. "Who told you that?"

"I overheard." My voice rose as if I were asking a question, not giving an answer.

Valentina clicked her tongue. "Sneaky little..." Her voice trailed off, but her lips continued to move.

"Did the funds truly save us from becoming destitute?"

She sighed. "Your father asked I not tell you for fear you'd put undue pressure upon yourself."

"I'd have done that anyway." I slumped against the headboard. Father was right—knowing about the money made it worse. What if I failed? My family would be required to repay what they'd already received. I couldn't allow that.

Calm yourself, Carola. First, just survive this trip.

My legs longed to escape the cramped coach and stretch. Just how far north was this flower worthy of such efforts?

I kissed the cross around my neck. *Father, please deliver me safely to my destination. Inspire me to paint a portrait that will satisfy my benefactor. And make my host amicable to Valentina and me.*

Why was I commissioned for such a work? Flowers weren't my forte. Nature's beauty moved me, but the downtrodden compelled my paintbrush to portray the hopelessness that shattered my heart, hoping those in lofty positions might be moved to act. This proved to be a fruitless endeavor. The nobles didn't care to display societal ills on their walls. I'd never support myself or my family with such glaringly prejudiced art.

The flower, on the other hand... I hadn't even painted it, and already it had provided all my family's needs while I was away with the promise of more to come once I completed the work.

Twinges pestered me like a hungry dog. I should feel nothing but gratitude, and yet I felt I was abandoning the underprivileged by accepting a sum to paint something so... inconsequential. By accepting this task, I played into the hands of the rich.

But I was helping my family.

At seventeen, well into marrying age, I'd already spurned several suitors. My choices were running dry. If I was to remain with my family much longer, I had to make it profitable for them, rather than drain their resources.

I'd work to support them for the rest of my life, but if that didn't work out, I'd become a nun. Nothing gave me greater pleasure than accompanying Mother Alma to hand out food to those in need. And I'd be allowed to paint, write, and continue my education.

Come what may, I wouldn't succumb to society's indoctrination that it was a woman's sole duty to desire a husband and children above all else. So many women suffered at the hands of their husbands. And if she should find herself barren or fail to produce a son? That was most unforgivable. No. Life offered far more important things than marriage and handling a household.

The carriage jarred, and I smacked my head against the backrest. I rubbed the sore spot, then uncovered the window to watch the trees rushing past. Riding into the unknown unnerved me, but it was only two months. Not a lifetime of marriage.

I stiffened. What if this was all a trick? A ruse to marry me off without my consent... The idea snaked within me, wrapping around my lungs, making breathing nearly impossible.

No. I laughed off the absurd idea, sweeping away the snake before it nested. My parents wouldn't have received funds. They would have paid a dowry. And they supported my decision to become a nun. The remaining funds received from this work would help pay the dowry to the convent.

I had to stop entertaining foolish thoughts and focus on my task—to paint a rare flower and tell its story. I kissed my cross again. With God, I would face whatever lay before me and live to tell the tale.

2

THE CASTLE

Do not fret, for God did not create us to abandon us.

— MICHELANGELO

e rumbled along the rutted drive and lurched to a stop. I studied my temporary residence from the safety of the carriage. A cross between a fortified manor and a quattro torre castle with angular towers loomed before me. The estate must've been glorious not too long ago. Now, the crumbling stone walls threatening to dislodge the overhanging bay windows were more in need of repair than the road.

The landscape had long since begun the slow process of swallowing the castle whole. Fir and cypress trees dwarfed the structure, negating its defenses. Sprawling vines obscured several windows. Shrubs, having outgrown their place, now defended their expanded territory with jagged branches, daring anyone with a blade to attack. Tall grasses and weeds, clumped together in ugly masses, lay in wait, ready to trip up trespassers.

This estate looked like something from my cousin's horrifying fables. It delighted him so to scare my younger sister and me out of our wits.

The eager anticipation previously bubbling within me burst, flattening like an uncorked and forgotten bottle of wine. If the exterior was any reflection of its owner, this would be a dismal stay, indeed.

The driver opened the carriage door and held back the curtain. I took his proffered hand. The coach jostled as I disembarked. Despite the driver's aid, my ankle twisted on the uneven ground.

"My apologies, madonna." He assisted me in righting myself, then released me to help Valentina.

"Watch your step." I tested my ankle. It smarted but seemed fine. Smoothing my wrinkled gown, I eyed the arched entryway across the stone drive.

The carriage creaked as Valentina emerged. She shielded her eyes to appraise the castle and grimaced. "Let's hope our host is simply too busy for upkeep."

"Allow me to announce you, madonna." The driver passed us with our baggage to the entryway and knocked.

The heavy wooden door groaned. A bald man with a scraggly beard poked his head through the opening.

Hand to his chest, the driver bowed. "Madonna Salviati for Messer Viviani."

Grunting, the bald man pulled the stubborn door wider, his gaunt face reddening with the effort. Rather frumpy, his tattered tunic and doublet hung on him, much looser than was fashionable. Perhaps he'd lost weight and had yet to have his tailor take in his clothing. And perhaps he'd lost his comb.

I clutched my cross and gave him a wide berth. A musty odor clogged my sinuses. A chill made me shudder as my eyes adjusted to the dank cobweb-strewn foyer.

The driver deposited our belongings on the worn carpet and tipped his hat. "I'll return to your father to announce your safe arrival, madonna." He sped away to his carriage. Even he couldn't wait to leave.

"I'll show you to your rooms." The nameless man grunted again as he lifted our baggage.

I curtsied. "Thank you, Messer—?"

"Bonavento."

I nodded and followed him through the stale hall. We passed several rooms, void of furnishings and boasting tattered carpets. Bare walls begged for paint—anything to brighten this dismal space. Where were the frescoes that cheered every home I'd ever greeted?

We continued following the servant up a circular stairway, coughing on the dust he kicked into our faces. Windows meant for security illuminated the grimy steps. After passing the second story, the repetition gave a sense of endlessly traveling upward with no hopes of arriving.

"Messer Bonavento, when shall we be introduced to Messer Viviani?" I asked.

"He'll introduce himself in his own time."

Did our host have no sense of decorum? No wonder his servant had such poor manners.

We followed the boorish man up three flights to a dim room where he delivered our things. With thick curtains blocking the window, sconces and lanterns offered plenty of light, and a warm fire crackling in the hearth cast dancing shadows along the walls as if attempting to put on a puppet show. Cozy *dust-free* furnishings promised respite, and the bedding appeared clean. I breathed in deeply of air scented with jasmine, and the mounting tension eased. Perhaps this stay wouldn't be so terrible.

"Might I ask why our rooms are so high up?" Valentina struggled to speak as she caught her breath from the climb.

"I was told to prepare rooms where you'd have the entire floor to yourselves."

How curious. Was our host conscientious, or had my parents made the request?

An easel awaited in the corner beside a table littered with art supplies near the only window. I riffled through them—an unused palette, brushes, and more colors than I had at home beckoned me. Either Mother had this sent ahead, or our host had gone through pains to select the right items.

"There's a cistern just off the stairwell and a latrine at the end of the hall." Bonavento opened another door. "Your handmaid may sleep in the adjoining room. There's no hearth, but if you leave this open, both rooms should get sufficient warmth. The cold season has ended, but the castle always has a chill. You'll find warming bricks beside the hearth should you so desire."

"I'm sure that won't be necessary." Valentina picked up her bag and carried it next door. "What of a bath?"

"Across the hall."

Drawing back the heavy draperies, I gasped. Night was nearly upon us, but it had yet to obscure the gardens. They must've been amazing to behold at one time, the likes of which kings would've taken notice. Despite years of neglect, the beauty in the artistic design remained. Terraced gardens led to a bricked path surrounding a rectangular pond overrun with algae. Mazelike hedges lined the paths where statues were placed with an artist's eye. Tall cypress trees rose above the crumbling walls. But, like the front of the castle, it resembled an ancient ruin.

What flower worthy of a portrait could exist among such negligence?

I clung to my cross as the insidious thought that this was some elaborate scheme infiltrated my mind once more. But was it possible? Had I been unwittingly sold off into marriage? Or worse... Had I been lured here by a well-funded madman?

3

A FRIGHTFUL HOST

The greatest deception men suffer is from their own opinions.

— LEONARDO DA VINCI

*V*alentina and I sat in the dark dining hall at the end of a long table. An iron chandelier with several spikes loomed overhead like a mouthful of teeth awaiting its meal—the guests. If the chain holding the contraption in place were to break, only those sitting at the corners would be safe. I pulled out my notebook and chalk to capture the lethal contraption.

Again, the walls were bare. Why would someone with no interest in art commission an artist?

I caught sight of a hooded cloak. The grim reaper? I leapt to my feet. My notebook tumbled to the floor, and my chalk skittered away. I gripped the back of the chair, ready to wield it should that prove necessary, and crossed myself.

The wraith removed his hood to reveal something far more frightening than the angel of death—an eerie face, like a porcelain doll with no facial features. A mask with cutouts for eyes, nostrils, and a mouth. A scream lodged in my throat. Nothing in my cousin's frightening repertoire could compare with this unholy creature.

My grip on the chair tightened as I considered fleeing the castle and taking my chances in the unforgiving mountains.

Valentina grasped my hand with a reassuring squeeze, but her face blanched. She stood and curtsied. I dipped a curtsy as well, smoothing my dress with shaking hands, averting my gaze from the eyeless holes.

"My lord," Valentina said, still bowed.

"There are no lords here," he grumbled.

Bonavento folded his master's cloak over the crook of his arm, and the man, whom I presumed to be Messer Viviani yet sincerely wished wasn't, took his seat. Did he plan to eat with that thing on his face?

"Forgive me, Messer Viviani." Valentina corrected herself.

"I don't care for such formalities. Those are for civilized society of which I have no part. Call me Soren."

My breath caught. How could I address a strange man so informally? And what did he mean, he had no part of civilized society? I dared lift my gaze to the vile mask. Was he admitting himself to be a lunatic?

Valentina and I sat, but I was rigid, ready to bolt at the slightest twitch. A maid served our meals—polenta taragna with trota salmonata. The fish didn't look entirely appetizing embedded in the speckled mush, but polenta was one of my favorite dishes. Though many nobles frowned upon polenta, thinking themselves above it despite our long history, for me, it brought fond memories of home. A welcome comfort in my time of need.

Our uncouth host clearly had funds, yet he didn't appear to have any trouble eating or serving the dish. Did that comfort me or make me warier?

Regardless, his lack of convention provoked my curiosity.

I lowered my defenses and scooped a small amount of food. The buttery cheese melted on my tongue, leaving behind the gritty texture of buckwheat and cornmeal that transported me to my childhood. Whoever cooked this dish was an artist in the kitchen.

"How do you like the fish?" our host asked. His voice sounded like rocks rubbing against a wood scraper. "I caught it from the river just this morn." He peeled the mask away from his face to allow his spoon access. From my vantage point at the table's far end with the light before him, I could see nothing of his face past the mask's shadow.

I tried the salmon trout. The crunchy skin and flaky meat were cooked to perfection. "It's very good, Mess —Soren." My face warmed, and I wished I had a mask. He'd asked us to call him Soren. As difficult as that may be, I'd have to get used to it. Lord or not, he was the master of this home.

Scraping spoons and clinking goblets echoed in the dingy hall. The silence pinched my every nerve. Meals were a time for conversation, not brooding. "When might I see the flower I'm to paint?"

"In due time. They're not yet in bloom... Carola, is it?" His voice made my throat sore.

I nodded, still uncomfortable with the intimacy of undressed names.

"Are you a writer as well as an artist? I'd like the story of how the Smeraldo flower came to be to accompany the painting."

I blinked. "Smeraldo? That's the first I've heard the flower's name." But smeraldo meant emerald. Was I to assume the flower was green? I'd never seen nor heard of a flower with green petals. But I dared not ask such an ignorant question and make him question his judgment in hiring me. "Perhaps you might tell me the flower's story then."

"In due time."

His repetition of that brush-off made my blood warm to a low simmer. "Am I not here to paint a flower and write a story? And yet you've neither a flower to show nor a tale to tell?"

"I'll not be pressed when it comes to matters close to my heart."

I blew out a frustrated breath. "May I ask how you found me? There's no shortage of more capable artists."

"I've no need for pompous fools and their pride."

"What makes you think I'm not a pompous fool?"

"I've seen your work."

Had he? My spine jerked to its full length. "Where? I've never sold any pieces, though I did donate some to Mother Alma." I raised an eyebrow. "Do you know Mother Alma? Have you visited the convent?"

He shoved his plate aside and stood. "If you'll excuse me."

While he bowed and stormed away, Valentina and I stared at one another. What had I done wrong? Was it the mention of convents? Was this further evidence that he was unstable? Just how long would I have to stay here—with this barbaric man and his horrid disguise?

4

CLEANING HOUSE

The greatest danger for most of us is not that our aim is too high and we miss it, but that it is too low and we reach it.

— MICHELANGELO

My stiff body resented being dragged out of bed the following morning. Every muscle resisted, accusing yesterday's ride for their sorry state. It didn't help matters that I hadn't slept well. The bed was comfortable enough, and our hosts had done a decent job cleaning our rooms. But this was a stone castle. Nothing could eliminate the musty air clogging my nose and stifling my breathing. And something scurried about our rooms all night. I'd woken several times to light my lantern and check the room, certain I'd find a rat—or a ghost.

I shivered both from the idea of rats in my bed and the brisk morning air. Gooseflesh broke out across my arms. Eager to get to the breakfast table and hear the flower's story, even from our unconventional host, I quickly dressed and freshened. Despite my hurry, Valentina was ready and waiting by the time I'd finished.

I nearly tripped on the stairs in my haste. But when we arrived, the table was empty with only two place settings—was that for me and Valentina or me and Soren?

"I should check the kitchens." Valentina turned to leave as Bonavento entered with a platter.

"Where is Messer Viviani?" I took the liberty of using his master's proper name in his absence. Our host never directed me to use his given name with others.

"Messer Soren has already broken his fast and gone to hunt pheasant." Bonavento thudded the platter before us, then rubbed his gnarled hands together. "If you should like to dine with him, you must rise before the sun." He forced a smile. "Is there anything else you should desire?"

"Will he return for the midday meal?" I asked.

"Not likely." Bonavento stood, staring.

I stared back for an uncomfortable minute. Then it dawned on me, I'd never answered his question. "Thank you, Messer Bonavento. That will be all."

Bonavento bowed and sauntered away as Valentina uncovered the lid to reveal a typical morning snack of white bread and cheese.

"Is that grana padano?" I reached for a chunk of the hard cheese and tested a bite, savoring the nutty flavor. It reminded me of the times before Father had lost an entire ship full of his wares at sea. Times when we could afford such a fine, aged cheese. And yet, it saddened me. I missed my parents. I missed the happier days with less worry. But guilt hammered away at me for enjoying such exquisite food while the poor struggled to calm their empty bellies. I returned the cheese to my plate.

"Oh, Carola, you bleeding heart. You're allowed to enjoy fine things when presented to you." Valentina knew me like no one else. "Should it grow moldy and unfit for rats?"

"Of course not."

"When you're a nun, you can serve the poor. For now, God has called you here. And when He gives you a gift, accept it with gratitude."

Valentina was right. She was always right.

I ate my gift, trying to block out the hungry faces I'd forever captured on my canvases and in my heart. Though eating without an unnerving mask watching me was rather pleasant, I remained eager to hear the story—to do my job—and return home.

"Why do you think someone with means lives with so few servants? Are there any others aside from Bonavento and the maid?"

Valentina shrugged. "I'm sure we'll learn soon enough."

We toured the grounds while waiting for Soren's return. Though the rest of the estate had been ignored for some time, someone gave the vegetable garden proper attention. It was the only area with fresh plantings and no weeds. Healthy artichokes, spinach, cabbage, and celery spread in abundance. Elsewhere, irises were in bloom, but like so many otherwise healthy perennials, weeds choked them out. Nowhere did I find any portrait-worthy flowers.

"Messer Viviani did say they weren't in bloom." Valentina picked up her skirts and climbed the stairs back to the castle. "I should make myself useful."

We found a broom and some dusting rags. I followed her, sweeping as she wiped away dust and cobwebs.

She opened the windows. "You don't need to do this, Carola. There are art supplies in your room. Didn't you want to paint the valley from our ride?"

"I'm too anxious for that right now."

She shrugged it off, and we spent the day cleaning with me constantly looking over my shoulder, waiting for Soren to appear so my real work could begin.

We made our way through the castle. On the far end, beyond the bare inner courtyard, stood a grand room with large windows overlooking the gardens. White sheets covered all the furnishings. Is that why the rest of the castle was so barren? Had most of the furniture been moved here?

This must've been a great gathering hall at one point. I imagined lords and ladies in their finest attire. The men blathering on about politics and conspiring to line their already thick pockets while the women prattled away about frivolous indulgences that mattered only to the rich.

I was glad this room was abandoned. "Should we ignore this one?"

She glanced about. "We could shake out the coverings and sweep the floor."

I groaned. Only Valentina would want to be so thorough.

We came to some crates in the corner and lifted the sheet. Valentina shook out her side, sending a spray of dust in my face, and I coughed.

"What's this?" I pushed the sheet aside and lifted a frame from the crate with care. A beautiful portrait of a woman. I replaced it and picked out another. The crate was full of artwork. "Why would someone commission me for art, when his are stowed away? Clearly, he has no appreciation."

"Don't judge." Valentina wagged a finger, and I let the subject drop, not bringing it up again even as we uncovered several more.

Once we finished the great hall, we moved to the sitting room, one of the few furnished rooms on the main floor. As I tugged back the curtains and dusted the windowsills, I passed the first piece of art I'd seen on the wall. An oil painting of an emaciated boy in tattered clothes holding out his hand, begging for food. I sucked in a sharp breath.

"What is it?" Valentina asked.

"It—it's mine."

She came to inspect. Her fingers brushed my name in the corner, C S Salviati.

5

SPIES

He who follows another will never overtake him.

— MICHELANGELO

I couldn't wait to question my masked benefactor about my painting, but as time wore on, I cared less about the art on his wall and more about the job from which my family had already benefited. Day after day, we sought after him to no avail. If Soren came and went, he did so before Valentina and I woke and after we retired. I fumed as I paced the length of my chamber. "Four days! He hasn't appeared in four days, Valentina. What am I to do if he never shows? My parents will have to pay back the money, and—"

She grasped my shoulders. "Tomorrow, we'll wake before dawn and follow him wherever he goes. Hunting, fishing. Whatever it may be, you will be there, and he can no longer ignore you."

A reasonable plan. Taking back some control relieved me. My pent-up energy fizzled away, and I nodded. "Tomorrow."

"Wake up, Carola." Valentina shook me.

I struggled to open my eyes. With Valentina like a ghost in the lantern's glow, I took a moment to realize she was standing there, fully dressed at this unholy hour. Then our plans came rushing back, and I leapt from the bed. We donned our cloaks and were ready to go in record time. It was still dark and eerily quiet as we stole from our quarters down the stairwell.

"Where should we wait?" I asked in a whisper.

"Outside where he won't see us."

"What if he goes out the back?"

"Then we'll wait out there tomorrow."

I groaned at the prospect of having to go through this effort again. But I followed her into the mist. "At least it will be easier to hide in the fog."

"Yes, but the fog may obscure him from us, too."

I clutched my cross. *Please, God, you know how much my family needs this. Don't let him escape me any longer.*

We stood behind a tree and waited. The gray of early dawn lightened the sky, and daring birds braved the dismal conditions, cheering it somewhat with their song.

"Where is he?" I asked. "Did we miss him?"

"Shhh!" Valentina pressed a finger to her lips as the telltale scraping of the heavy front door sounded.

We ducked behind the tree, circling it while Soren marched past. When he was far enough away, we followed at a distance. Despite the fog, we trailed him to a village where he disappeared inside a modest stone building. A church? Valentina and I sidled up to it, ducking under the windows.

"Are you here for food?"

I jumped at the voice at my back. A young boy with a dirty face stood there with a smaller girl, equally as unclean.

"Forgive me. I didn't mean to give you a fright," he said.

"It's quite all right." I patted my chest as if that might reset my heart to its proper rhythm. "Is there food here?"

The boy nodded. "I've never seen you before."

"We're visiting... a friend."

He scrunched his face as if he didn't believe anyone would purposely visit anyone else around here. "If you're hungry, come inside. The man who feeds us looks scary—"

The little girl placed a hand beside her mouth and spoke in a loud, yet hushed voice. "He wears a mask."

The boy grasped her. "Come on." He pulled the girl around the corner and disappeared inside the building.

More voices sounded as others arrived, narrowing their eyes when they passed us.

"What should we do?" I eyed my expensive clothes, wishing I had worn something less... noble. But I didn't own such clothing.

Valentina huffed. "The girl who helps Mother Alma distribute food is asking *me* what we should do?"

We stepped inside the dingy building. Rows of benches filled the meager room. A line of people along the wall skirted the seats. Soren stood in the back of the building. He shoved a roll and a pouch into people's hands as they went by.

Just who was this man? Cold, distant, yet he distributed food to the poor? And he hung one of my portraits prominently in his home—the only piece of artwork in the place.

People waiting stared at us and whispered to one another. Valentina ushered me into the line. No one spoke to us. Nor did I know what to say to them. I'd always been the one waiting with food to hand out, ready with an encouraging smile. Being on this side felt... strange, especially since I was an impostor with no need of food.

When it was my turn, Soren had a roll ready to place in my hand. But I didn't reach for it. Instead, I stared at his mask. Yet again, he stood in dim lighting, and I failed to see his eyes beyond the holes. But the eerie visage moved from my hand to my face. "*You*. You followed me?"

"You gave me scant choice." I would not feel shame nor guilt for taking action when he left me in a lurch. But now was not the time. He had people to feed. "What can we do to help?"

He cocked his head at me. Did he always place himself so nothing about his face could be seen? He pointed to a door across the room. "Go see Father Domenico."

In the back room, we found a man in priestly garb dragging a basket of rolls.

"Father Domenico?" I asked.

"Yes." He released his load. The basket tipped, and a roll tumbled away. Valentina scrambled to catch it. "Can I help you, my child?"

"I'm Carola Salviati. This is my handmaid, Valentina. Messer Viviani suggested we come see you. That you might show us how we can be of assistance."

He wiped his brow. "You're not one of my parishioners."

"No. We're Messer Viviani's guests."

"Oh?" That seemed to pique his interest. "Would you care to fill pouches with corn?"

"Of course." I smiled, eager to do something useful.

"Would you like me to bring those rolls out to Messer Soren?" Valentina asked.

Father Domenico beamed. "If it's not too heavy, I would appreciate that greatly."

She dragged the rolls out the door.

"Have a seat." He motioned toward a table littered with pouches.

From where I sat, I could watch Soren handing out food. I stared, memorizing the setting. The way the light streamed in through the windows, stretching out in misshapen rectangles on the parishioners' heads, across the tiled floor, over the wooden benches, and illuminating one side of Soren's mask. The gaunt faces, some haggard, some hopeful—all reaching out to the hideous man with no way of reading his expression. There was something disturbing, yet beautiful in the scene. Unlike the majestic mountain view that may never make its way to canvas, this would.

Soren's mask turned my way—I'd been staring. My cheeks warming, I returned to my task, not daring to look up again. He must be laughing behind that hideous doll face.

"May I ask how it is you're acquainted with Soren?" Father Domenico opened the sack of corn and handed me a scoop.

"He commissioned me to paint the Smeraldo flower and tell its story." I scooped corn and filled a sack.

"Did he?" Raising a brow, he sat across from me and joined me in filling the sacks.

"Yes, but he's done little to assist in that matter. He disappears early each morn and returns late at night." I was getting into an enjoyable rhythm with my work.

Father Domenico nodded as if he expected nothing less. "I must confess, I'm amazed he commissioned such a work. Soren has come a long way in these past years, even daring to venture beyond our humble village to the cities to gather more supplies for our people. But I don't know that he's spoken of that flower with anyone except for me. I'm sure he's not eager to relive the pain."

Pain? Curiosity burned within me, eager to glean more, but it would be inappropriate to pry. I sighed. "But he must. My family has already been paid much of the commission. I can't return home until my work is done. Might you convince him, Father?"

He sighed as though he already knew it was a wasted effort. "I will see what I can do."

Valentina stood in the entryway. "Would you like me to take over, Carola? Messer Soren could use some help distributing the food, and I know how you love to do it."

I hesitated, then nodded. Perhaps I'd have an opportunity to speak with him.

"Here, bring these sacks of grain."

We helped Father Domenico arrange the filled sacks into the basket, and I carried it to Soren. After he placed a roll into every open hand, I offered them grain, and the familiar yet inexpressible joy came bubbling up within, though my sorrow for these people's misfortune diluted it somewhat. I longed to do something more. But I was doing something. It wouldn't solve the bigger problem, but it would satisfy their hunger for the moment. And their smiles and appreciation satiated *my* hungry soul. I smiled at Soren. At this angle, with the way the light streamed through the window, I could see his eyes smiling back at me.

6

THE MAN BEHIND THE MASK

To know each other is the best way to understand each other. To understand each other is the only way to love each other.

— *MICHELANGELO*

*V*alentina and I trailed Soren through the woods to the castle. She nudged me, imploring me with wide eyes and a nod in his direction. I shook my head, not wanting to push. I was exhausted as he must be, and our return trip was mostly uphill. My thighs burned, and my lungs preferred I not waste their effort on idle chatter. Our mission was a success, provided Soren didn't escape again.

Bonavento was waiting for us when we arrived. He took our cloaks, then disappeared.

"Perhaps I might assist in the kitchens," Valentina said.

Before I could convince her to rest, she was rushing away. Her shoes clacked across the tile floor, echoing through the hall until they disappeared.

"Did someone clean?" Soren asked. This was probably the first time he'd seen the place in daylight since we'd arrived.

"There was little else to do with you gone." I huffed.

He turned to me. "You?"

Though I was growing accustomed to his eerie mask, his gaze made me uncomfortable. "And Valentina."

"Thank you."

Talk of cleaning reminded me. "I found one of my paintings in your sitting room."

When he clasped his hands behind his back and made his way to the dining hall, I chased after him.

"How did it come to find you? It's one I donated to Mother Alma."

He shrugged. "She gave it to me."

"Why?" Despite the part of me that was hurt she'd give away my painting, I was more curious as to what he was doing there and why he wanted my artwork.

"I appreciate your work."

"No one appreciates my work."

"Am I a liar then?" He wheeled around. I nearly collided with him, halting within inches of his chest. He smelled like eucalyptus. "And if you believe such nonsense, why do you paint?"

I had no answer. How could I explain the feeling that came over me when something caught my eye, moved my emotions, and made my hands itch until the scene was captured on canvas? A desire—no, a *need* —to share that vision would not allow me to rest until it was forever portrayed in paint. And I hoped my works might turn hearts and help viewers *see*—even if such a fruitless endeavor would never support my family. There was no explaining it other than to shrug and say, "I have to portray what moves me."

"And you think no one else could be moved by such things?"

"Well, I—I haven't met many who care to see the poor at all, never mind displaying a constant reminder on their wall."

"I"—Soren took a deep, sorrowful breath—"*need* to remember." He turned back around and pulled out a seat for me at the dining table. Perhaps he had manners after all.

"How'd you come to be at the convent?" I asked.

"I trade with Mother Alma." His clipped speech made it clear he didn't care to speak of the matter any further.

Bonavento served us stewed pheasant and wine—an excellent pairing. Valentina placed a domed platter of fruits and cheeses on the table and joined us to eat.

I'd nearly finished my meal, and Soren had hardly spoken. Valentina prodded my knee beneath the table. I made a face at her, then asked Soren, "Does the Smeraldo grow elsewhere in Italy? Or the world?"

He shook his head. "There is only one place it grows."

How peculiar. "And it's on this property?"

"Would I invite you here to paint it if it were not?"

I bit back an equally sarcastic retort about luring me here for more nefarious motives. I would get my story, come what may. "How is it you've come to live here—alone? Do you have any relations?"

"None of consequence."

I scoffed. "Does family mean nothing to you?"

Soren's glass clunked on the table, and a drip of wine sloshed over the edge. He motioned for Valentina to go. "Leave us."

She nearly toppled her chair in her haste to comply, her head vacillating between Soren and me.

Once she was out of earshot, Soren said, "My family rescued me, and I'm indebted to them. But the illegitimate son of a duchy is a liability, not a valued family member."

I gasped. Son of a duchy? I wanted to ask who but thought better of it. "But your family provided all of this, did they not?"

"My father protects and provides for me to satisfy his guilt."

I found myself at a loss for words.

Soren leaned over the table, his frightful mask closing in. "I trust you'll keep this information to yourself.

Until my father has a rightful heir, my life is in danger. He's taken great pains to hide me from the world and to ensure the few who know of my existence believe me dead."

"You're in line for the duchy?"

"No. Nor do I want it. The duchy should go to someone more capable of the task as opposed to a masked man."

"You could remove the mask."

"That would be worse." He reached under his mask and swiped at his nose. "What I'm about to tell you has no part in the story, not until my father has passed and his estate has been distributed. Understood?"

I nodded. My heart pattered, daring to believe now might be the time to pry the story from him.

"My father had an affair with my mother, his gardener's daughter. Though I have no legitimate claims as my father's heir, someone feared that might change. They torched my home in an attempt to kill me."

"Who?"

Soren spread his hands. "A member of my father's first wife's family, I presume, though I'll never be certain. I know of none other who'd have wanted me dead other than one with a desire to ensure I'd never lay claim to my father's estate. My father took advantage of the situation and made it appear as if I'd died along with my mother. Then he hid me here."

I scarcely breathed. "How old were you?"

"Seven."

My heart squeezed like grapes in a press for the boy within the man in the mask. "I'm sorry to hear of your mother." I held a hand over my heart as if I could hold it back from spilling over. "Were you burned? Is that why you wear the mask?" I'd likely prefer to look upon whatever disfigurement he suffered, to look upon the human than speak to a featureless doll's face incapable of expression.

He nodded. "I grew up here with Bonavento and my servants. He's the only father I've ever known."

"Where are your servants?"

"Other than my cook and Zita, a girl who comes to clean sometimes, I have none left. I released them, six years ago."

"Why?"

"We'll get to that later."

I took a deep breath and tried not to let the brush-off discourage me. I *was* getting answers. "Where did you receive your education?"

"I had tutors."

"Did you have anyone else? Friends?"

"No."

"You must've been lonely."

"I was. And once, when I was young, I so longed for a friend, someone my age, I made the mistake of venturing into the village." He scoffed.

"Oh no." I covered my mouth with my hand. "What happened?"

"My servants were paid not to react, so I didn't realize the extent of my hideous disfigurement. But those boys ensured I understood. That was when I commissioned my first mask."

Though his story tugged on my heart, I must proceed with caution. Bullying and isolation tended to produce miscreants, not pious men. He was an orphaned, isolated, disfigured victim of attempted murder. A perfect recipe for a madman.

"But even with the mask, the people in the village didn't accept me. So, I remained here. Every once in a while, some young boy would appear on my land. The victim of a dare by his peers. I heard what they said about me." He pulled the mask away to sip his drink. "Forgive me for being so forward."

"There's nothing to forgive. I'm here for this story."

"It's not so much that all this is part of the story. But I'm hopeful that, if you understand my circumstances, you'll understand what happened to the young woman."

Young woman? I gulped. What had he done?

THE FLOWER THIEF

Love shows itself more in adversity than in prosperity; as light does, which shines most where the place is darkest.

— *LEONARDO DA VINCI*

*S*oren fiddled with the stem of his wine glass. "I found joy in gardening, especially flowers. One night, when I was barely a man, fifteen years at most, I sat in my garden, enjoying the cool night sky after the heat of the summer's day. A young woman about my age, dressed in rags, jumped over my wall and picked my flowers. Stunned, I wanted to shoo her away, but I wasn't wearing my mask. Instead, I hid and watched her pluck my prized possessions, filling her basket to the brim, then disappear back over the wall from whence she came.

"Who was she to steal my hard work? I planned to lay in wait for her the next night with my mask. But the next day, during my studies, I happened upon a scripture about not gleaning the edge of your fields, but rather, leaving it for the poor and the stranger. Are you familiar with that passage?"

"It's in Leviticus." I appreciated his asking rather than assuming me to be uneducated, as men tended to do. "But there's a difference between allowing the poor to glean what you leave unharvested and outright thievery." My heart softened toward him as I spoke. So many quoted the Bible, yet so few truly attempted to follow its teachings, especially where justice was concerned.

"Yes, but I decided to find out what she was doing before confronting her. She looked poor. And if she had need of my flowers to survive, what was that to me? They wouldn't feed me. Gazing upon their beauty wouldn't sustain my life."

"So, what did you do?"

"The next night, I extinguished my lanterns and pretended to go to sleep, but I hid, lying in wait, hoping she'd return."

"Did she?" I asked.

"Yes. Just before she descended the wall, she paused, peering at the house. The moonlight caught her face, and her beauty mesmerized me. I can still see it." His voice thinned as he stared off, beyond me. He cleared his throat and returned from his reverie. "She picked my flowers, yet I made no move to stop her."

"Did you follow her?" I asked.

"Not at that point. I had planned to. But I suspected she'd go to the village, and I wasn't ready for that. Instead, I found myself doing the same thing the next night, snuffing out the lamp, then watching, waiting. And again, for several nights.

"With each passing night, my curiosity grew until I no longer cared if she led me to the village. I wrapped myself in my cloak, donned my mask, and followed her through the village to a shack in the woods. From what I could tell, she lived alone with an ailing mother. I slept in the trees that night. Then, in the morning, she went into the village to sell my flowers. The money she received was probably all that was keeping her and her mother alive." His voice cracked, and he took another sip of his drink. "Her name was Lia."

My heart broke for the girl. And too many girls like her. She was probably too poor to marry or even join a nunnery. Both required dowries. Such injustice. I clenched my fists.

"I longed to help her. To teach her to grow the flowers for herself so she could earn a decent living. But I couldn't show her my face. Even with the mask, I frighten people. Perhaps more so. And I couldn't bear it if she never returned.

"Though we were both young, we weren't too young to marry. I would have married her without a dowry. But she could never love—or even pretend to love—someone like me. So, I decided to create something new, a flower that didn't exist elsewhere, something she might sell for a high price and live well. I shut myself away inside my castle, working diligently. After countless failed attempts, I found success."

"The Smeraldo flower," I said.

He nodded. "The buds stay closed during the day, but at night, when the moonlight shines down upon them, the petals open and glow like sparkling emeralds. I filled my garden with them, then waited for her return. I couldn't wait to see her reaction. The first person to set their eyes on my creation."

"And?" I leaned forward. "What did she think?"

He slumped in his chair. "She never saw them."

"Why?" My stomach sank as if he weren't merely telling a story, but it were happening now. I wanted to leap from my seat and help him find the girl, afraid of what he might say next.

"In my preoccupation with creating a flower to save her, I hadn't noticed my garden was bare. She'd taken all my flowers, and I hadn't grown more." Soren took a weighty breath while I scarcely breathed. "I waited night after night. Finally, I dared venture into the village to inquire after her. She... and her mother... both were dead." The fire in his voice died as if there was no air to fuel it.

I reached a hand out, wanting to soothe his pain, then thought better of it, and placed it on my lap.

"If I'd only inquired after her sooner..." He bent forward, covered his mask with his hands, and wept.

8

TENDING THE GARDEN

Perfection is no small thing, but it is made up of small things.

— MICHELANGELO

*S*oren left the room. When, after an hour, he failed to return, I made my way to the gardens. I scanned the area, imagining how beautiful it must've been once and how it might look again, with a little work.

I moved to the blooming irises, hiked up my dress, and knelt. Pebbles from the stony walkway embedded themselves into my stockings as I ripped away weeds and dead overgrowth to give the flowers room to grow. Once that section was clear, I continued on, revealing tiny green shoots poking through the soil. All this life, just waiting for someone to help it along. Encouraged, I buried myself in the task, continuing to work with no shears and no gloves.

"What are you doing?" Soren's voice startled me—I'd been so engrossed in my task. His eerie mask over my shoulder and his disdaining tone didn't calm my nerves.

I clutched my chest with a dirty hand, leaving a smear. "I'm just—"

"Where are your gloves? Have you no sense?" He squatted beside me and grasped my hands.

My heart seized as he swiped away soil and inspected my palms. I dared look at him. This close I had a good view of his eyes through the holes. The deepest brown, like burnt umber. Kind.

"Just as I suspected. Blisters." He released me and rooted around in his pocket.

Bits of mottled pink flesh were visible between his collar, his curly brown locks, and his mask. Did his skin look like that all over? Did it look worse than the mask? He dropped a pair of gloves beside me, then walked away.

I stared after him, then donned the gloves.

Moments later, he appeared with a loaded wheelbarrow. I continued my work, taking sidelong peeks as he unloaded pruning saws, knives, and a cushion.

He dropped the cushion beside me. "Kneel on that to spare your knees."

"Much obliged." I bowed as he loaded my refuse pile into the wheelbarrow and carted it away. Once he was gone, I readjusted myself onto the cushion. My knees appreciated the relief.

When he returned, he knelt beside me and cut away the dead branches I'd been unable to yank.

After several hours, I stood and stretched. My legs locked up, and my back screamed at me to never hunch over again. But I admired our work. One section of the garden was clear. It held nothing but potential now.

"If only I'd not been such a coward."

I'd nearly forgotten he was there until he spoke. And his comment confused me, seemingly coming from nowhere. Then I remembered the story. "Are you referring to the young woman? Lia?"

"I should have tried. Perhaps I could have saved her. But I shan't ever know. And she's dead... because of me."

Decorum be hanged. I seized his gloved hand. "It was not your fault." All this time, I'd feared he might be a murderer only to find he considered himself to be one—and falsely so.

"If only I'd told her the truth about how I felt. She might've accepted me. If not me, perhaps my help. She might've lived."

"You didn't kill her, Soren."

"I might as well have."

"Are you God?" I squeezed his hand. "Do you have the power over life and death?"

I couldn't see his eyes through his mask at this angle, but I could feel his gaze.

"Then it wasn't your fault." I eyed him, realizing the importance of what I was commissioned to do. "Your story must be told. Perhaps others who hear such a woeful tale will be moved to step outside their comforts to help another. Lia's unfortunate death may lead to more lives saved."

"That was my hope... that no one else should suffer as I have suffered. Or Lia..."

"Then I shall do my best. I will tell your story. But there's still one unanswered question."

He stared, waiting.

"Why did you release your servants? A garden this size needs tending. You should have a gardener. And the castle needs maintenance, cleaning."

He slumped his shoulders. "After Lia died in her poverty, I couldn't bear to be wealthy. I did nothing to deserve it. So, I tried to live as if I were poor."

"So, you let your staff go, taking work away from the people?"

He looked away.

I couldn't fault him. Grief causes peculiar behavior. So, I changed the subject. "When might I see the flower?"

"In about a week, the first blossoms should form."

I glanced about the gardens. "Is it any of these sprouts?"

"The Smeraldo flower doesn't grow in these gardens anymore."

I narrowed my eyes. Even after his tale, I couldn't help but question if I was being tricked. Was there even such a flower? "Then where?"

"Elsewhere on my property." He must've sensed my suspicions. "In due time, when the flower is ready, I will show you."

WE SPENT the mornings the following week tending to the garden until all the weeds and overgrowth were gone. I hoped I'd remain long enough to see it in all its fullness.

Valentina joined us when her self-imposed schedule allowed. She'd taken to filling in wherever needed—running errands in the village, tending vegetables in the gardens, assisting in the kitchens, cleaning... There was nothing that woman couldn't do.

In the afternoons while there was still sufficient daylight, I sketched and painted Soren in his mask handing rolls to the poor. He'd moved my easel onto the courtyard and, every once in a while, would appear over my shoulder to check my progress. Each day, he would stroll through the gardens, then disappear through the door in the back wall.

The Smeraldo flowers must be through that door.

But today, he departed after the midday meal and had yet to return.

"They're ready."

Startled, I nearly painted my artwork with an unfortunate streak of Venetian red. I caught myself before ruining my painting and spun around. "Soren, you gave me a fright!" Without thinking, I thrust my paintbrush at his mask, leaving a Venetian-red smear on its cheek. My hands flew to my mouth as I considered too late what I'd done.

"Did you—?" His finger found the blotch of paint and came away red. "You painted my mask."

"I'm so sorry. I—" I spoke behind my hands, horrified.

Soren swiped his red finger at my face. When I jerked back before he made contact, he laughed. "Oh, stop fretting. You'll get paint on yourself." He plucked the brush from my fingers and laid it on the table. "It's just a mask. I have others."

"Still, I—I don't know what came over me."

"Retribution." He removed a handkerchief from his pocket. "I don't fault you. I'd likely have done the same." He wiped his stained finger, making his handkerchief appear bloody.

Then he caught sight of my painting and gave it a double take. His fingers hovered over his masked face with light streaming in on him. I'd even managed to capture the kindness in his eyes. "It's remarkable."

"Thank you." I neared to show the finishing touches I planned. "It's not quite finished. I—"

"I don't look like a monster. How did you—" He turned to me, his face so close nothing more than a sheet of paper could fit between us.

We both jumped back as though stung by a bee.

I pressed my warmed cheeks as if I could push away the blush.

"I, uh..." He resumed cleaning his finger though no more paint came off. "I wanted to tell you that they're ready."

"What?" Then I understood and my breath hitched. "The Smeraldo flowers?"

He nodded. "Tonight will be a full moon. After the sun goes down, you will see them in all their splendor."

9

THE GRAVE

Beauty perishes in life, but is immortal in art.

— LEONARDO DA VINCI

After the sun retired and the moon took its place, Soren led me through the garden to a cluster of vines along the back wall surrounding the wooden door. He pulled a large key from his pocket and unlocked it. We continued along a pathway.

"I set up your easel and paints with several lanterns that I hope will offer sufficient light."

So this was what he'd been doing in the afternoons while I painted. It appeared freshly weeded, lined by a row of perfectly trimmed shrubs. I followed him through a vine-covered arbor to a clearing. An unearthly green glow shimmered in the distance, and I sucked in my breath. A mound of flowers shone like emeralds. Something lay at the head of the mound. A stone.

A gravestone.

"Is this—?" A sob lodged in my throat.

"Lia's grave." He knelt and touched one of the flowers as if it were made of glass. "She was to receive a pauper's funeral. I couldn't have that. Since she had none to claim her, I did. I gave her a suitable resting place with a proper headstone. I hoped my flowers might bring her comfort."

If she hadn't been buried yet, he must've missed her dying breath by mere moments. From his story, I'd been under the impression that it had been much longer. "What of her mother?"

"She had passed away several weeks prior. I don't know what became of her body. Lia might've buried her somewhere herself."

Tears slipped down my cheeks. This life was cruel to the poor. Lia may have known nothing of Soren, his love for her, or the Smeraldo flowers. But her body rested on his grounds, and sparkling emeralds blanketed her grave. Moved by a heart that would do such a thing, I wanted to see the man behind the mask. I knelt beside him and reached for his mask, then caught myself. "May I?"

He stiffened. "May you what?"

"I want to see your face."

"No, you don't."

"Like you can't appreciate my art?"

He laughed.

"Please, allow me."

He sighed, shaking his head as if already regretting what he was about to do, then reached up, and removed the mask. Puckered skin ran along one side of his face from his forehead, past his cheek, then disappeared beneath his neckline. One eye drooped slightly. Still, the scarring wasn't nearly as bad as I'd expected. The other side had some scruff along his angular jaw and upper lip. I gazed into his dark eyes, glistening from unshed tears in the moonlight as I raised a hand and touched his rough cheek.

His eyes closed at my touch. Tears slipped from beneath his lids. Whatever had been percolating in my heart for this man now permeated all of it.

His eyelids fluttered open, and horror lay there. He scrambled to his feet and out of reach. "How can you, an artist, stand to look upon such a grotesque disfiguration?"

I stood slowly, as if not to frighten a cornered animal. "I think the world has distorted your mind more than the fire has distorted your face."

He scoffed and backed away, shaking his head. "No one could love this face. No one." He stalked away down the path.

"Soren, I—"

The door slammed behind him, and I stood there, my arms heavy at my sides, helpless. Should I follow? He'd taken off his mask. That was a breakthrough, wasn't it? Perhaps he needed time. I should just leave him be.

Taking a deep breath, I turned to the easel. My hand itched, not to paint the flower, but Soren's face as I saw it. Perhaps then, he'd understand. But that's not what my family was paid for me to do. And I needed to fulfill my duty. So, I summoned all the emotions swirling within me—my disappointment at his retreat, my sorrow at the lies he believed, and my anger at the world for twisting his mind. They pumped through my heart where I allowed myself to feel the pain. Then I trapped my emotions there, tapping into them to feed my hands as the brush made its way across the canvas.

AT BREAKFAST THE NEXT MORNING, Bonavento advised Valentina and me that Soren had left on business. But he couldn't look me in the eye as he spoke. He must be lying. What business would Soren have to attend to?

"Where has he gone?" I asked.

"Florence, I believe."

Such a long trip? "When will he return?"

Bonavento grunted. "I have no way of knowing. A week? A month?"

My stomach clenched. We'd be gone within a month. Was he doing this to avoid me? Had he holed himself up somewhere in the castle, hiding from me as he'd hid from Lia? Something was growing between us, knitting our hearts together. Didn't he feel it, too?

Perhaps it was one-sided. Or perhaps the damage the world had done to him, convincing him love was an impossibility for him, was irreversible.

"Has he gone to visit Mother Alma?" I asked.

Bonavento shook his head. "He merely stated he had business to attend in Florence, nothing more."

AFTER THE SUN went down that eve, I carried two lanterns to Lia's grave. I hung one in a tree and balanced the other on a table. I'd sketched the scene the night before and gave it finishing touches while I still had daylight. But I had to wait for them to bloom to observe their true color. It was rather troublesome that they only opened at night. What colors should I mix to mimic this unearthly green? And how could I imitate such radiance with mere paint?

Valentina situated the two lanterns she carried on the ground. "Will that be enough light?"

"It will have to be." Now that the full moon had passed, I had precious few nights in which to work as each night would offer less and less light. Even now, their radiance seemed more subdued than the night before.

Although I was only commissioned to paint one painting, I wanted to paint two. One close up on the flower alone and another of the entire mound with the gravestone lit by the moonlight.

I mixed my paints, summoned the loss I felt from Soren's absence, and swiped the canvas with brush strokes meaningless to anyone else. To me, it was as if the painting already existed, I merely needed to bring it to life.

I TRIED NOT to feel the lack of Soren's presence the next day as I painted what I could without the flowers open.

Valentina came down the path with a glass of water. "How's the painting coming along?"

I groaned and took a long sip. "I can't get the color quite right, and I don't know how I'm going to depict their glow."

"You can do it, Carola." With a smile, she turned to walk away.

As I looked down at the glass in my hand, an idea struck me. "Wait, would you fetch me a few things?"

"Such as?" she asked.

"A hammer." I thought about all I'd need. "A cloth, a bowl, a strainer... and a pestle and mortar."

Valentina cocked an eyebrow at me, then left. When she returned, I tossed the remains of my water, dried the glass with the cloth, then wrapped the glass in the cloth, and set it on the ground.

Just as I raised the hammer, Valentina stopped me. "What are you doing?"

"You'll see." I brought the hammer down, smashing into the glass. Something was oddly satisfying in the act. I readjusted the cloth, then swung again and again until only shards of glass remained. Then I settled the strainer inside the bowl and shook out the broken fragments. I shook the strainer until I had a sufficient amount of glass bits, then poured it into the mortar and ground it into a powder with the pestle.

"What do you plan to do with that?" Valentina asked.

"Paint with it." I smiled, eager to experiment. I mixed the glass powder into the blend of colors I hoped did justice to the true flower. I held the brush in the air for a moment to pray.

Please, God. Don't let this destroy what I've already done.

Valentina peered over my shoulder as I worked and gasped. "Carola, you've done it! Look how it shines!"

I stepped back to survey my painting. My heart skipped like a carefree child. I had done it.

If only I could show Soren...

10

HOMEBOUND

As you give out, so shall you receive.

— MICHELANGELO

*N*ight after night, I worked. Day after day, I inquired after Soren with no news. It saddened me. Not for myself, but for him and for the life sure to pass him by if he couldn't get past his demons. He believed himself too hideous to be loved. But little did he realize, I lived in a world full of truly hideous men. Perhaps not on the outside. But, in my experience, the better the outward appearance, the worse the interior. I would rather become a nun than subject myself to the ugliness within them.

For the first time, I'd met a man who was beautiful where it mattered. A man I could see myself enjoying life with, tending gardens with, and raising children with beautiful souls in their father's image. And I could have captured our lives on canvas.

But, if Soren's misguided heart was never brought to rights, that vision would never be.

By the time I finished both paintings and wrote the Smeraldo flower's story, the gardens were in full bloom. I wished for time to paint them. But Soren had yet to return, and my family was expecting me. The work was complete. And, therefore, so was my reason to remain.

While I waited for word as to when I'd be leaving, I painted his face as I recalled it that night, his kind burnt-umber eyes shining in the moonlight. It was my best work yet, and I wanted him to see it. But he hadn't returned. Or come out of hiding, whichever the case may be.

Valentina entered my room carrying her packed bags, dressed in her traveling clothes. "The carriage should arrive shortly." She glanced about, then sighed as she began gathering my things. "How is it you're not packed?"

"I've been busy." I cleaned my brushes.

"Are you stalling?" She fetched my bag from behind the chair.

"No. My work is done. Nothing's keeping me here."

On her way back to the things she'd deposited onto the bed, she glimpsed the painting on the easel and sucked in a sharp breath. "Is that Soren? You saw his face?"

As I pressed my lips together, she studied the painting. "Does he know you're in love with him?"

"Ha! I most certainly am not." I rolled my brushes in their pouch and stashed them inside the bag.

"He removed his mask for you, yet you're still hiding behind your artwork."

Had the woman gone mad? "What on earth are you saying?"

Valentina sat beside her pile on the bed. "You've never opened yourself up to love, though I'm at a loss as to why. Unlike Soren, you have no visible scars, nor do you hide behind a tangible mask. But it's there all the same. It's as if"—she narrowed her eyes and pinched her fingers together as if straining to see the idea they held—"long ago you decided all social constructs were born of man's ignorance and swore never to fall prey to them. Now you can't allow yourself to break your misguided vow."

Fury boiled within and erupted. "Soren ran away, not me!"

"And what if he'd stayed, Carola? Would you have accepted him had he asked?"

I blew out a steamy huff and flopped into the chair. "I don't know. I—I guess I'll never know."

THE CARRIAGE ARRIVED to take me home. Though Soren still hadn't returned, I had no choice but to leave. Valentina's words nagged me, the truth to them chafed like tight chopines. But now, I think I would've liked the chance to see what life with Soren would have been like. He shunned the frivolities of the rich as I did. And he also cared for the poor. We could've worked together to come to their aid, to advocate for them. What might we have done together?

The idea that I might never know pressed upon my heart like a hot iron. With our bags packed, I had no further reason to stall.

Valentina put a hand on my shoulder. "Ready to go?"

I wasn't. I didn't think I'd ever be ready to go. But I had no choice. Unlike Lia, I wouldn't die. I would be content as a nun. It was a good life—perhaps not the life I might've had with Soren, but a good life nonetheless. Soren wouldn't have another death on his conscience.

As Bonavento collected our bags, Valentina and I carried my paintings and followed him out of the room that had been my home for the past two months. I'd never expected to feel such fondness for it after such a short time.

Bonavento hung my work in the foyer for Soren to see the moment he returned—the flower's close-up, the flowery grave, and Soren unmasked. We stood back and appraised them.

"They came out beautifully, Carola." Valentina patted her heart. "If only your parents could see them. Your use of color and addition of glass to make the petals appear luminescent is brilliant."

"I haven't seen Soren's face since he was a boy," Bonavento said.

"Your best work yet." A tear slipping down her cheek, Valentina pressed her fist to her heart.

I stiffened and blinked back tears.

Bonavento gave me a long look as if he wanted to say something, then changed his mind. He squeezed my shoulder and gathered our things.

Please, God. If you intend me to marry Soren, please help him. Bring him to me.

After that short prayer, I expected Soren to appear. To chase after me—unmasked. I kept looking over my shoulder—once the bags were loaded, after Valentina boarded, and as I climbed the steps. I parted the curtain and stared out the window, expecting him to come barging out of the castle.

But he never did.

Bonavento closed the carriage door, then paused in the window. That same look came over him, like he wanted to say something. "Master Soren, he–he cares for you."

Before I could form a thought into meaningful words, he banged on the carriage, signaling the driver that all was ready. But *I* wasn't ready. My heart split, and a piece remained behind. The pain grew with the separation as the coach jerked to a start and I swayed in my seat.

Whether he cared for me or not, he never came. My disillusioned heart learned a harsh lesson in reality—feelings were of little consequence without action. The castle disappeared in the foliage, and I buried my face in my hands and sobbed.

MY TEARS DRIED as I braced myself against the jostling. I couldn't both cry and protect myself. The carriage jerked to one side, throwing me into Valentina, then came to a stop. I peeled myself from her girth.

"Did we hit something?" I peered out the window. Mountains and fir trees filled my view.

A gloved hand reached through the curtain, fumbled with the lock, then yanked the door open. A masked face peeked inside.

"Soren?"

His gaze caught mine. "Were you leaving without showing me the painting?"

"They're in the entryway. You can see them anytime."

"They?" He shook his head. "Not without you."

"You've had plenty of opportunity, yet you're stopping us now?"

He cocked his head. "I've had no opportunity."

"What do you mean? You—"

"I've been away, attending to business. Didn't Bonavento tell you?"

"Yes, but—" I stared, speechless.

He glanced at Valentina's frozen expression, then turned to me. "Do you mind coming out to speak with me a moment?"

I descended the steps to the view I'd seen on the way to his castle, the very spot I'd wanted to stop and paint. I gaped at it now, unobstructed.

Soren grasped my hand and eased me away from the carriage. "Carola, I'm just returning from Florence. I had to inquire after a certain young lady's father.

Though some complications delayed me, my venture proved fruitful."

"I don't understand." I shook my head. "What are you trying to say?"

He dropped down to one knee and removed his mask.

I sucked in a breath.

He wasn't—

This couldn't be—

"Carola, I've made all the financial arrangements and received your father's blessing, but I want to know— Could you stand looking upon this face for the rest of your life?" He cringed as if expecting a negative response.

I would have said yes before. But now, watching him in broad daylight remove his mask and show true courage to ask such a question... And to have ventured to Florence to speak with my father? I was more in love with him than ever. I touched his scarred face. "Yes, Soren. I would love to look at you for the rest of my life."

He flinched as if I'd said no, then cocked his head. "Y–you'll marry me?"

"Yes." I laughed.

He jumped to his feet, wrapped his arms around me, and lifted me into a spin. He lowered me and, as the world continued to spin, brought his lips to mine. A jolt ran through my body, and I knew there was no man for me—other than this one.

SHAMELESS REQUEST FOR REVIEWS

Authors need reviews! They help books get noticed, and I love to know what my readers think of my stories. So, if you enjoyed this book, please consider leaving a review wherever you purchased this book, Goodreads, BookBub... everywhere and anywhere you think a review might be helpful. I'm forever grateful!

You are loved,

J F Rogers

ABOUT THE AUTHOR

 J F Rogers' permanent residence is in Southern Maine with her husband, daughter, and pets, but she often travels to fantastic worlds with whatever imaginary characters are lurking around. She has a degree in Behavioral Science and teaches a 5th & 6th grade Sunday School class. When she's not entertaining Tuki the Mega Mutt, her constant companion and greatest distraction, she's likely tap tap tapping away at her keyboard, praying the words will miraculously align so you can visit her worlds, too. Above all, she's a believer in the One True God and can say with absolute certainty—you are loved.

Connect with J F Rogers

jfrogers.com

 twitter.com/jfrogers5

instagram.com/jfrogers925

bookbub.com/profile/j-f-rogers

pinterest.com/jfrogers925

A jaded elf. A feisty dragon. And a deadly curse that threatens them all.

Samu would do anything to be bonded to a dragon, even serve a king he doesn't trust. But when a strange mist falls over his city and the humans massacre the elves, the last thing he wants is to come to the king's rescue.

Then the dragon eggs are threatened, and the Divide grows dark.

This was no ordinary curse.

Someone... or something... is staging an extinction-level attack against the elves and their dragons.

But Samu won't let that happen. He can't. He'll rescue the dragons or die trying.

The Darkening Divide is the action-packed prequel to The Cursed Lands Christian fantasy adventure. If you enjoy mixing up genres with elves and dragons in a steampunk world infested with humans, download The Darkening Divide today! You'll love this intro to J F Rogers's exciting new series.

http://jfrogers.com/free-book/

Astray

A mysterious amulet leads Fallon to everything she's ever wanted...and possibly her death.

Adrift

Fallon returns to Ariboslia to save lives...but the creatures she wants to save want her dead.

Aloft

Fallon and Morrigan face off for the ultimate battle ... in their minds.

Alight

Three friends. Evil seeks to corrupt them. If they survive... what will it cost?

THE CURSED LANDS SERIES

The King's Curse

A king with a god complex. A people without free will. Can Colleen save their doomed souls?

The Witch's Curse

Colleen must face her fears to free those under the witch's curse... or remain trapped in her nightmare forever.

The Queen's Curse

Coming February 2024

Still looking for more?

Be among the first to know when new books are released. Join her clan today!

jfrogers.com/join/

ACKNOWLEDGMENTS

As always, I must thank God first. Everything comes from Him, including my daughter, who I must credit next. If not for her love of K-Pop, I wouldn't have written this story. She introduced me to many groups, grilled me on their names, dragged me to New York for several concerts, and made me watch countless music videos, interviews, song lyric videos, and shows such as Run BTS. Which leads me to... BTS.

I must thank BTS though they will never know how they inspired me. They're an incredible group of talented artists. Many of their songs move me, but none so much as The Truth Untold. What a heartbreaking song! Then I learned the lyrics were based on an Italian folktale, *La Cittá di Smeraldo*. I hunted it down, hoping to read the original tale.

But I found none.

It shouldn't have surprised me that there were no written tales to be found aside from brief stories with little more than major plot points. Folktales were handed down orally and many never make it to paper. But I wanted more.

So I wrote one.

I must thank Julie Bernier. The long chat back from our writing group meeting fueled this story. I couldn't wait to write it after that conversation. The first draft practically wrote itself.

I'd also like to thank my husband for always being supportive and reading the terrible first drafts; my fantastic critique partners: Jan Davis Warren, and Damascus Blades: C W Briar, Gina Detwiler, Katherine Massengill, Laura McCary, and Alexander Preston; the best editor, Dierdre Lockart; 100 Covers for your incredible cover art, Rene Klein for your invaluable feedback for the cover design, my beta readers: Noel Armstrong-Wade, Jenny Cardinal, Angel Cross, Debbie Harris, Laura G. Johnson, Birgit Lehmann, Bill Long, John Parus, and Monique Summers; and my clan—you give me a reason to write. Thank you so much for your feedback on the cover and your continued support and encouragement.

Emily—This story is dedicated to you. I make it sound as if I'm a victim of your K-Pop phase. But I loved all the time I spent with you. Thank you for giving me an appreciation for music in different languages. And thank you for your support and insight for this story. I'm so blessed to have such a wonderful daughter.

BTS Army—If you, like me, sought this folktale only to be disappointed, I hope The Smeraldo Flower satisfies that craving.

To those unfamiliar with BTS—give them a listen. If nothing else, listen to The Truth Untold.

To everyone—I hope you enjoyed reading this retelling as much as I enjoyed writing it. The Smeraldo Flower differs from my longer fantasy novels, but it was great fun to research and write.

God bless you all!

You are loved,

J F Rogers